DINOSAUR DREAM

written and illustrated by DENNIS NOLAN

Macmillan/McGraw-Hill School Publishing Company
New York Chicago Columbus

With thanks to Judith Whipple, Cecilia Yung,

Matthew, Lauren, Rudy Zallinger,

and to the memory of

Charles R. Knight who started it all.

Macmillan Publishing Company
866 Third Avenue, New York, NY 10022
Collier Macmillan Canada, Inc.

The text of this book is set in 14 point Bembo.

The illustrations are rendered in watercolor.

For information regarding permission, write to
Macmillan Publishing Company,
866 Third Avenue,
New York, NY 10022.

This edition is reprinted by arrangement with
Macmillan Publishing Company.

Macmillan/McGraw-Hill School Division
10 Union Square East
New York, New York 10003

Printed and bound in Mexico.
ISBN 0-02-274913-6

1 2 3 4 5 6 7 8 9 REY 99 98 97 96 95 94 93 92

For my mother,
who introduced me
to my first dinosaur

Wilbur climbed into bed and opened his favorite book, *Through the Ages*. He turned the pages back through time, past ancient cities, past the great Ice Age and the Age of Mammals, and past the Cretaceous period when *Tyrannosaurus rex* prowled. At last he found what he was looking for, a picture of a long-necked dinosaur nibbling the top of a tree. "*Apatosaurus*, also known as *Brontosaurus*," he read, "from the Jurassic period, over one hundred forty million years ago." He studied the picture until his eyelids grew heavy and he turned out his light. Then came a tapping at his window. Softly he crept across the floor and stared into the black night. A pair of bright red eyes stared back, and Wilbur jumped away in fright.

Wilbur looked out the window again. Standing in the soft glow of moonlight was a baby dinosaur swishing its long tail through the grass. It can't be... thought Wilbur. Gently he opened the window to the warm night air. The dinosaur just blinked its eyes. "My very own dinosaur," said Wilbur as he put on his slippers and climbed out the window. "Just wait till I tell everyone. I'll put you in the barn with Greta. I'm sure she won't mind. She's just a cow." He coaxed the dinosaur to the barn and quickly shut the door behind it. Immediately it began to howl, waking up Greta and all the chickens. The barn was in an uproar of mooing and clucking until Wilbur finally let the dinosaur out. "This won't do at all," said Wilbur. "I'd better take you home."

Wilbur led the dinosaur across the pasture toward the woods. "This is no place for a dinosaur, anyway," said Wilbur. "You would get lonely here with no other dinosaurs around. And besides, pretty soon you will outgrow the barn. I will take you back to the Jurassic period where you belong." He hugged the dinosaur as it thumped its tail on the ground. "You need a name," said Wilbur. "I will call you Gideon, after Gideon Mantell. He discovered the first dinosaur fossil." Wilbur turned and walked into the shadows of the woods. "Follow me, Gideon," he said. "We have one hundred forty million years to go through."

Wilbur led Gideon through the woods, over bubbling brooks, and past tall swaying trees. "I've never been this far before," he told Gideon. "I hope it's the right way." The hoot of an owl sent a shiver down his back. Gideon's eyes grew bigger and glowed bright red in the black of night. With another shiver, Wilbur realized it was beginning to snow. "But this is summer," Wilbur said. "It's not supposed to snow! We *must* be going back through time." Soon they were trudging through snow up to their knees. Gideon whined as the night grew colder, and they struggled to the end of the woods.

The sun was just beginning to rise when Wilbur and Gideon reached the edge of a giant glacier. They stood motionless as a herd of huge shaggy animals moved slowly through the heavy snow. "Gideon," Wilbur whispered, "those are woolly mammoths! This must be the Ice Age!" Gideon snorted. A mammoth stepped forward and swung its twisted tusks into the air. It sent a long, trumpeting noise echoing through the valley. Gideon squealed, but Wilbur grabbed him around the neck before he had time to run off. The mammoth turned and led the rest of the herd quietly away. "Come on, Gideon, we'd better be going, too," said Wilbur. "We're back a long way, but not far enough."

They marched out across the glacier as icy winds whipped about them. Gideon ran from the wind and tried to hide among the boulders, only to find a hungry saber-toothed cat clawing at the ground and flashing its long sharp fangs. "Here, Gideon, quick!" cried Wilbur. They scampered up the rocks to safety. "Next time stay with me, Gideon," said Wilbur. Gideon's teeth chattered as he trembled more from fear than from the cold. "Don't worry," said Wilbur, petting Gideon. "Soon we'll be out of the Ice Age and into the Age of Mammals. At least it will be warmer there. I just hope we're still going the right way," he muttered to himself as they headed for the high mountains.

It was not long before Wilbur and Gideon left the Ice Age far behind. Brightly colored birds sang and huge black butterflies fluttered overhead. The day was growing hotter as they climbed higher into the mountains. Finally Gideon stopped by an icy stream and drank from the clear water while Wilbur looked for a shady spot to rest. "We've been walking for hours," he said, "and we haven't found anything yet. This must be the wrong way." He was almost ready to turn back when a tiny horse scampered up the mountainside in front of him. "Look, Gideon," he cried, "a dawn horse from fifty million years ago! We're in the Age of Mammals at last! This *is* the right way!" Gideon squealed with delight and chased the dawn horse up the rocks. "Not so fast, Gideon," Wilbur hollered after him. Gideon ran back to Wilbur, licked his cheek, and together they walked up the mountain.

The sun beat down as they stood on the mountaintop and gazed out at the land below them. Mighty volcanoes rumbled, sending rivers of sizzling lava down their sides. Pools of hot mud bubbled angrily, and steam rose from cracks in the earth. Gideon paced about nervously. "Come here, Gideon. Look." Wilbur pointed to the giant-winged reptiles floating silently in the warm breeze. "Those are *Pteranodons*. That means we're in the Cretaceous period, sixty-five million years ago. It can't be far now," said Wilbur. Gideon sniffed at the hot air. A steep path led straight down the mountain. "Climbing down might not be so easy, though," said Wilbur, examining Gideon's clumsy looking feet. "You'd better stay close behind me." Step by step they slowly inched their way down the rocks toward the thundering volcanoes.

Gideon and Wilbur followed the winding path down the mountain. Far ahead lay a wide green valley dotted with shimmering lakes. "Maybe that's the Jurassic period down there," said Wilbur. Then he saw some *Triceratops* sleeping peacefully in the sun. "Oh, Gideon," he whispered, "I *have* to get a closer look." But Gideon would not leave the path. "They won't hurt you, they're asleep," said Wilbur and finally convinced Gideon to follow. They crept slowly toward the gigantic horned dinosaurs. One opened a sleepy eye and suddenly rose to its feet. It snorted and began to charge. Wilbur and Gideon escaped into the cliffs. "Sorry, Gideon, this time it was my fault. Well, we're safe now," said Wilbur as they rested on a rocky ledge.

All at once the earth shook and the mountains echoed with a terrifying roar. Gideon looked, and shuddered at the sight. A monstrous *Tyrannosaurus rex* was leaping across the rocks toward them. It swished its long tail in the air and chomped its heavy jaws. "Faster, Gideon," yelled Wilbur as they ran from the enormous dinosaur. The *Tyrannosaurus* was nearly upon them when they came to a swift river that bounced wildly around sharp boulders. There was nothing left to do. Wilbur grabbed Gideon and jumped into the cold water. They were swept away by the churning rapids while the fearsome *Tyrannosaurus* pawed angrily at the banks of the river.

Hanging on tightly to Gideon's neck, Wilbur kicked against the strong current. But it was no use. They were pulled to the edge of a high waterfall. They screamed as they fell through the crashing foam, just missing the slippery rocks below. The splashing waters carried them down to a wide green valley. Finally they scrambled to shore. They collapsed on the warm bank and let the afternoon sun dry them off. Wilbur lifted his head drowsily. "I don't know if I can move another step. What about you, Gideon?" Gideon lay snoring among the ferns. Then the earth trembled, and they both jumped to their feet. A group of enormous long-necked dinosaurs ambled toward them with great plodding footsteps. Gideon sniffed the air and wagged his tail. "We've found it! We've found the Jurassic period," Wilbur cried out as they ran across the fields of ferns to meet the Apatosaur family.

Wilbur and Gideon spent the rest of the afternoon happily wandering across the valley with Gideon's family. Soft summer breezes circled about the great beasts as they nibbled the tops of the tall trees. Wilbur watched a *Stegosaurus* browsing among the ferns and *Archaeopteryx* gliding from branch to branch, while Gideon splashed through shining creeks and chased giant dragonflies. The sun set behind the mountains, and all too soon the day was over. Wilbur hugged Gideon tightly. "I wish I could stay," he whispered. "But it's time for me to go home." Gideon blinked his red eyes and licked Wilbur's cheek. Waving good-bye to Gideon and the rest of the herd, Wilbur began his long journey back alone. Soon he was joined by the biggest *Apatosaurus*. The enormous dinosaur knelt before Wilbur, who climbed on its back, happy for the ride home.

Pteranodons let out their last cries of the day and soon the sound of rumbling volcanoes filled the air. The *Apatosaurus* climbed high above the valley as Wilbur thought about his trip through time. He remembered the freezing winds of the Ice Age and the scary saber-toothed cat. He thought about the mighty *Tyrannosaurus rex* and the ride down the waterfall to the valley. He smiled as he remembered Gideon chasing dragonflies through the ferns. He missed Gideon already and decided he would visit him soon. It will be easy next time, he thought, because now I know the way. Wilbur yawned and snuggled comfortably on the back of the *Apatosaurus* while it moved gently through the mountains. Long before they reached his house, Wilbur was fast asleep.

T I M E   C H A R T *

QUATERNARY PERIOD

0–2
Million Years Ago

ICE AGE TO PRESENT

Woolly Mammoth

Woolly Rhinoceros

Saber-Toothed Cat (Smilodon)

TERTIARY PERIOD

2–65
Million Years Ago

AGE OF MAMMALS

Glyptodont

Uintatherium

Dawn Horse (Eohippus or Hyracotherium)

CRETACEOUS PERIOD

65–136
Million Years Ago

LAST AGE OF DINOSAURS

Pteranodon

Tyrannosaurus Rex

Triceratops

JURASSIC PERIOD

136–190
Million Years Ago

AGE OF DINOSAURS

Stegosaurus

Apatosaurus (Brontosaurus)

Archaeopteryx

*Not drawn to scale, all dates approximate